MAMA'S MORNING

by Kate Sternberg

ADVANTAGE BOOKS

Mama's Morning   by Kate Sternberg

To
Bob
Ryan Max
Pat Q. Della
Cathey Laura
Julie Jani
and Grandma Toppy

Library of Congress Cataloging-in-Publication Data

Sternberg, Kate, 1954-
    Mama's Morning / by Kate Sternberg.
        p.   cm.
    Summary: One hectic Monday morning overworked Mama Hamster has a great deal
of difficulty getting her four active children ready for school, and they are quite
surprised when they do arrive.
    ISBN 0-9660366-0-3
    [1. Morning--Fiction. 2. Hamsters--Fiction.   3. Mothers--Fiction.
4. Family life--Fiction.] I. Title.
PZ7.S838946Mam 1998
[E]--dc21 --dc21   97-41105
                                                                              CIP
                                                                               AC

Copyright © 1997 by Kate Sternberg
Published by
ADVANTAGE BOOKS
4400 East-West Hwy, Suite 816, Bethesda, MD 20814

Manufactured in the United States of America
10 9 8 7 6 5 4 3 2 1

Every morning before he goes to work, Papa kisses Mama and says, "Wake up, Honey. You have a busy day ahead."

A few minutes later, Mama kisses us and says, "Wake up, Hannah, Holly, Howie and Harry. It's time to get ready for school. Don't forget to make your bed."

As we eat breakfast, we help Mama plan the day. Mondays are the hardest. We have a lot of activities after school.

"Don't forget, Mama, I have ballet today," says Hannah.

"Gymnastics for me," says Holly.

"Band practice in Bob's garage," says Howie.

"Then karate at four," says Harry.

"Please, Mama, don't forget to pick us up on time."

Mama says she will, but we still make a big note to remind her.

The phone rings, and Mama answers it. While Mama talks, she starts some chores. She never, ever does one thing at a time. While she's busy, we sneak in some cartoons.

"What are you doing?" says Mama, when she finally gets off the phone. "I can't believe you children are watching TV when you are supposed to be getting ready for school."

Every morning we have to wash our faces and clean our ears.

We comb our hair and brush our teeth.

"Oh, dear!" Mama says. "We're out of toothpaste. I know I saw a coupon for that new brightening kind here somewhere."

Mama gets distracted easily. If we don't help her find that coupon now, she will just keep looking and looking and forget what she's supposed to be doing. Sometimes Mama forgets where she puts things, but she never forgets to thank us for finding them.

"Look at the list. It's time to get dressed," says Mama. "Make sure everything matches."

"Where are my pink tights with the sparkles?" asks Hannah. "I hope you washed them, Mama. I need them for ballet today."

"Did you sign my permission slip for the gymnastics field trip yet, Mama?" asks Holly. "I gave it to you Friday. If I don't turn it in, I can't go."

"Has anyone seen my glasses?" asks Howie. "I thought I left them on the sink, but they're not there. Mama, please help me find them."

"Oh, Mama. I forgot to tell you I need two dozen sunflower seeds for a party at karate today. It's Master Cashew's birthday, remember?" says Harry.

"Help," says Mama. "I can do a lot, but I can't do <u>everything</u> at once. I'm not Supermom!"

We come to Mama's rescue, just like our favorite heroes would.

Hannah whirls through the wash.

Holly plows into the paper pile.

Howie does some heavy lifting,
and Harry kicks bud.

In the middle of all the excitement, Mama says, "Oh, my goodness. Look at the time.

School starts very soon. Don't forget to bring your backpacks and tie your shoes."

Trying to run as fast as we can, we all trip over somebody's untied shoelace.

Mama says, "Why do I always have to remind you children to do everything?"

"Mama, we have to remind you to do stuff, too," says Hannah.

"You always forget to sign our permission slips," says Holly.

"You're usually the last parent in line to pick us up," says Howie.

"Mama, where's our lunch?" asks Harry.

"Oh, dear," says Mama, "I was so busy, I forgot to make it."

Good thing Mama is a champion gardener. Maybe we're old enough to make our own lunch.

"Bye, Mama," we say, with four quick hugs. "We'll miss you."

"I'll miss you, too," says Mama.

All along the path to school, we don't see any other friends. Maybe that sign on the door can tell us why.

How could we have forgotten? There's no school today. Now we have the whole day to play.

Maybe Mama can take the day off, too.

MAMA'S OUT playing

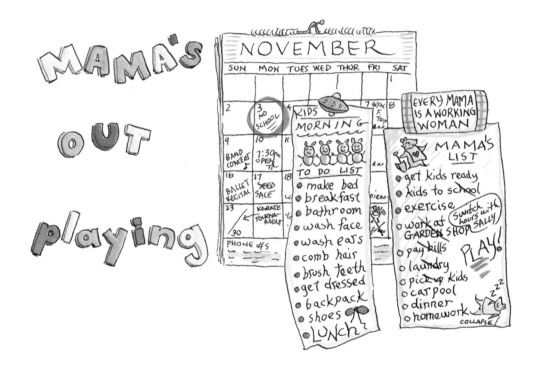